CUMBRIA LIBRARIES

3 8003 05196 2892

KT-434-853

2 3 SEP 2021

This book is on loan from
Library Services for Schools
www.cumbria.gov.uk/
libraries/schoolslibserv

Cumbria
County Council

The big red suit was ironed and ready.
The elves had stuffed the final teddy,
When from the bathroom came a yelp,
"Ho ho, oh no! Quick, someone HELP!"

The elves dashed in there in a hurry,
"Whatever's wrong? We're here, don't worry . . ."
But one elf made a squeaking sound
When Santa slowly turned around.

"I did the most **ginormous** cough
And shaved my famous beard right off!
The children won't know that I'm me,
We can't let anybody see."

"We'll fix it!" cried the worried elves.
They rifled through the workshop shelves.

You've seen the toys that elves can make,
A beard would be a piece of cake.

"We'll stick the bits back on with glue,
Your beard will look as good as new.

Or maybe not. Come on, elves, *think* . . .
Let's try the bubbles from the sink!"

It looked like it might work at first,
But one by one the bubbles burst.
The kitchen elf came running in,
Alerted by the awful din.

"Some squirty cream will do the trick!"
But Rudolf ate it with one lick.
Elves were racing round and round,
Grabbing anything they found.

The snow beard melted
straight away.

The workshop cat just wouldn't stay.

Mashed potato wasn't right.

Candyfloss was pink, not white.

They knitted an amazing one –
A beard with sparkles just for fun.
But it gave Santa such a tickle,
He got into an awful pickle.

"Nothing works, I'll have to hide.
I can't go out like this," he sighed.
"Unpack the sleigh, we're staying here,
There'll be no Christmas gifts this year."

But in the barn, someone was busy,
A teeny tiny elf called Lizzie.

She took the reindeer from each stall
And, with permission from them all,

She snipped a bit of pure white fluff,
The really soft and silky stuff,
From every reindeer's stubby tail.
This had to work, she couldn't fail.

She sewed and sewed without a break
(Except to nibble Christmas cake).
And underneath the setting sun
The elf sat back, her work was done.

When Santa saw, he clapped and cheered,
"You clever elf, a brand new beard!
Repack the sleigh, it's time to go.

Happy Christmas, ho ho ho!"

To keep the reindeer's bottoms warm,
Now that their fluffy tails were shorn,
Just look what Mrs Claus had done . . .

Christmas pants for everyone!

That tiny elf who saved the day
No longer sweeps the reindeer hay.

She's Head Inventor – now you know
Who helped make Rudolph's red nose glow!

You boys and girls are clever though,
And know that beards take time to grow.
So if you visit him this year,
And have a chance to get quite near,

Before you do a double take,
And shout, "That Santa's beard is fake!"

He might have done a giant cough
And shaved his famous beard right off . . .